To Phoebe Silver, who loves snow leopards

Special thanks to
Rachel Elliot

ORCHARD BOOKS

First published in Great Britain in 2018 by The Watts Publishing Group

1 3 5 7 9 10 8 6 4 2

© 2018 Rainbow Magic Limited.
© 2018 HIT Entertainment Limited.
Illustrations © Orchard Books 2018

HiT entertainment

A CIP catalogue record for this book is available from the British Library.

ISBN 978 1 40835 504 6

Printed and bound in Great Britain by CPI Group (UK) Ltd, Croydon, CR0 4YY

MIX
Paper from
responsible sources
FSC® C104740
www.fsc.org

The paper and board used in this book are made from wood from responsible sources

Orchard Books
An imprint of Hachette Children's Group
Part of The Watts Publishing Group Limited
Carmelite House, 50 Victoria Embankment, London EC4Y 0DZ

An Hachette UK Company
www.hachette.co.uk
www.hachettechildrens.co.uk

Selma
the Snow Leopard
Fairy

by Daisy Meadows

ORCHARD

www.rainbowmagicbooks.co.uk

Fairyland Palace

Sparkle Forest

Snow Leopard Enclosure

The Girls' Cabin

Elephant Bath

TAIL AND TRUNK SAFARI PARK

Jack Frost's Spell

I want a zoo – don't say I'm wrong!
But finding pets takes far too long.
Fill each cage with stinky straw.
I will get what I'm wishing for!

In Sparkle Forest every day,
Peculiar creatures run and play.
The animals are rare – so what?
Get in there and steal the lot!

Contents

Chapter One
Daybreak at Tail and Trunk

Rachel Walker opened her eyes. It was still dark in the room she was sharing with her best friend, Kirsty Tate.

"What woke me up?" she wondered.

As if to answer her question, she heard a few clear, beautiful notes from outside the window.

"The dawn chorus," Rachel told herself, smiling.

"Are you awake too?" came Kirsty's voice from across the room.

Rachel sat up and turned on her lamp. Kirsty hopped out of bed and came to sit beside her.

"Did the birdsong wake you up?" Rachel asked.

"No, I had a dream that we didn't find Dotty," said Kirsty. "We had to leave Tail and Trunk Safari Park without helping the fairies."

She shivered, and Rachel gave her a hug.

"That sounds more like a nightmare than a dream," she said. "But it's not going to come true. We'll find Dotty before we leave today. I'm sure of it."

The girls had won a night and a day at the safari park in a competition. Then they had persuaded Rachel's parents to stay for a few more days. They had been enjoying visiting the park with Ahmed, their guide, and helping to look after the animals. They had also been sharing a magical fairy adventure. Jack Frost had stolen the precious baby animals that

belonged with the Endangered Animals
Fairies. They had managed to find
three of them, but Dotty the baby snow
leopard was still missing.

"I don't feel tired at all," said Rachel.
"Let's watch the sun come up, and then
we'll think of a plan to start searching
for Dotty."

The girls kneeled up and opened the
curtains above Rachel's bed. The first
light of the day was so white and bright
that they had to turn away. But the
room was bright and white too.

"There's a light coming from behind
the dressing table," said Kirsty in
astonishment.

As if dawn was breaking inside the
room, the light grew brighter. Then
Selma the Snow Leopard Fairy appeared

at the top of the
dressing table.

"I'm glad you're
both awake," she
said. "I'm sorry it's so
early, but I've come
to ask for your help."

Selma shook
back her golden-
brown hair. She was
wearing jeans and a
summery green top
with brown boots.

"We'll do whatever
we can to help," said Rachel at once.

"Dawn and dusk are the best times to
see snow leopards," Selma said. "That's
why I thought it would be a good idea
to start searching early. Will you come

to the snow leopard enclosure and help me?"

"Of course we will," said Kirsty.

Quickly, the girls got dressed. Selma skipped into the air and flicked her wand. A shower of silvery sparkles rained around the girls.

"I feel as if I'm fizzing all over!" cried Rachel in delight.

Giggling, the best friends shrank to fairy size as their fairy wings appeared. They flew around the lampshade a few times, practising their dives and loop-the-loops.

"Being a fairy is the best," said Kirsty, plumping down on Rachel's pillow.

"Come on," said Rachel, pulling her into the air again. "Dotty needs our help."

Chapter Two
Spotting Dotty

The three fairies zoomed out of the window and into the fresh morning air. The safari park was quiet. No visitors were allowed in this early, and most of the keepers were still in bed. Every now and then, a peacock let out a shrill cry. Everything else was still.

Rachel and Kirsty flew over the animal habitats.

"It's funny," said Kirsty. "At the start of the week, the safari park seemed like a big maze. Now I feel as if I'd know my way around it with a blindfold on."

"That's because you've been helping to take care of the animals every day," said Selma. "Looking after animals and their habitats is the best way to get to know them."

"There's the snow leopard enclosure," said Rachel, pointing down to the waterfall at the centre of the enclosure. "But I can't see a single snow leopard."

The rock walls around the waterfall were rugged and steep. They looked as bare and grey as the walls of Jack Frost's Castle. But Selma smiled.

"Look again," she said. "Snow leopards are good at hiding."

They flew closer, and suddenly Rachel glimpsed a rock with black spots all over it. Then she realised that it wasn't a rock at all.

"Oh my goodness," she said, laughing. "It's a snow leopard. I didn't know they were so good at blending in with the background."

"They're amazing at camouflage," said Selma in a proud voice. "But I wish Dotty wasn't so good at it. I can't see her here."

Just then, a loud voice broke the peace of the morning.

"Coming, ready or not!" it squawked.

"That sounds exactly like a goblin," said Kirsty.

A green head peeped around one side of a pointy rock. From the other side, a fluffy white cub tumbled down, landed silently and scrambled away.

"Look at the tips of that cub's fur," said Rachel. "They've got a blue sparkle."

"Could that be Dotty?" Kirsty asked.

"It is Dotty," Selma exclaimed. "I'd know her markings anywhere. A snow leopard's spots are unique — just like our fingerprints."

She dived down towards the little cub, but Dotty disappeared. The goblin leaped down to stand beside Selma.

"Lost something?" he asked, cackling with laughter.

"Where is Dotty?" Kirsty said, landing next to Selma.

"Hiding," said the goblin. "She's playing hide and seek with me."

Just then, a thick, white tail poked up from the rock behind them. It gave a shy wave.

"Found you!" shrieked the goblin. "Here, kitty kitty. Would you like a saucer of milk?"

"She's not a pet cat," said Kirsty.

"Dotty, it's me," called Selma.

Dotty jumped on to a rock and gave a happy, rumbly purr. But before Selma could reach out to touch her, she had leaped away again.

"She thinks we're playing a game," said

Rachel. "Dotty, please come to us."

Dotty bounded off in the opposite
direction.

The fairies and the goblin chased after
her. She scrambled up rocks, jumped
across the waterfall and slid down a slope.

She had her mouth a little open, and her eyes were sparkling.

"She looks as if she's smiling," said Selma.

"She's having a great time," Kirsty panted. "But I wish she'd stop and listen."

Dotty raced around a large boulder and disappeared from sight.

"Follow her!" called Selma.

The fairies whizzed around the boulder and *THUMP!* They flew straight into someone in a long, flowing cloak. Dizzy and surprised, they fell to the ground with a bump. Selma dropped her wand.

"Got you!" shouted a loud voice.

They looked up to see Jack Frost grinning at them. Dotty was tucked under one of his arms. He scooped up Selma's wand and clutched it in his fist.

"Now we can have some fun," he said.

Holding the tiny wand in his fingertips,
Jack Frost waved it around wildly. Sparks
of fairy dust fizzed from it.

"My wand isn't supposed to be used
like that!" Selma cried. "Let me have it."

"Oh yes," said Jack Frost. "I'll let you
have something!"

Chapter Three
Fairies in a Pickle

There was a bright flash of light that
made blue spots dance in front of the
fairies' eyes. When they could see again,
their hearts sank. They were inside a
silver cage, and the gaps between the bars
were so small that they couldn't even put
their arms through.

"Let us go," Rachel exclaimed.

"You can't make him," sang the goblin in a mocking voice.

Suddenly there was a low growl, and the big snow leopard prowled around the boulder.

"He wants to know what's happening," said Selma.

"Clear off," shouted Jack Frost. "Shoo!"

He flapped his cloak at the snow
leopard. It snarled, and Jack Frost gave a
high-pitched squeal.

"Time to get out of here," he said.

There was a loud crack and a bright-
blue flash. Then the peaceful enclosure
suddenly vanished. The cry of the
peacock stopped. A cold wind whistled
around the fairies.

"Where are we?"
asked Rachel,
shivering.

Their cage
was lying on
its side in a soft
bank of snow.
Above them,
snow clouds filled
the air. Below and all

around was a sea of white.

"Welcome to the Blue Ice Mountains," said Jack Frost.

"We've been here before," said Kirsty with a burst of hope. "This is where Alyssa the Snow Queen Fairy lives. I'm sure she'll help us. Alyssa! Alyssa!"

"Shouting won't help you," said Jack Frost. "The Blue Ice Mountains are huge, and that silly snow queen fairy lives miles away. No one will ever find you!"

He threw back his head to laugh and bumped it on an icicle, which broke off and fell down the back of his cloak.

"YOWCH!" he shouted, hopping around in alarm. "That's nippy! Get it out of my clothes!'

As he reached up to pull out the icicle, he dropped Dotty. At once, she jumped

up and darted away.

"Get her!" he yelled.

Jack Frost and the goblin charged off after Dotty. Selma sank to the floor of the cage and covered her face with her hands. Kirsty hurried to give her a warm hug. Rachel was still standing beside the bars of the cage.

"It's no use," said Selma. "I'm so sorry, Rachel and Kirsty. We're trapped."

"Maybe not," said Rachel.

There was excitement in her voice. She pointed to something long and thin lying in the snow.

"It's your wand," she told Selma. "I saw it drop out of Jack Frost's hand when he was dancing around to get the icicle out."

"But how are we going to reach it?" Selma asked, sniffing. "We can hardly get our hands through the holes in the cage."

"Maybe I can help you," said a friendly

voice above them.

They looked up and gasped. A beautiful white bird was perching on the top of the cage. His feathers were as fluffy as duckling down. His eyes were turquoise, and a little crown of white feathers swayed on his head.

"Hello," said Kirsty in a gentle voice.

The bird opened its beak and sang a few sweet, liquid notes. Then it fluttered to the ground and bowed to the fairies.

"Welcome to the Blue Ice Mountains," it said.

33

Its voice made Rachel think of jingling bells. It made Kirsty think of bubbles. Selma stood up and curtsied to the bird.

"Rachel and Kirsty, this is a magical snowbird," she said. "They are very rare. I have never seen one before. Hello, snowbird. My name is Selma."

"I am Silentwing," said the snowbird. "When I saw Jack Frost and his goblin, I got worried. I knew they were here to make trouble."

Quickly, the fairies explained what had happened. Silentwing picked up the wand in his beak and passed it through the bars of the cage to Selma.

"Thank you," she said, smiling.

She shook her wand, and sparkling fairy dust fell on the lock of the cage. At once, the door flew open. Rachel, Kirsty and Selma fluttered out.

"If we're going to catch up with Dotty, we need to be warm," said Selma.

She flicked her wand, and the three fairies were suddenly wearing fluffy white onesies, covered with black spots.

"Now we look like snow leopards," said Kirsty in delight.

"How can we thank you for helping us to escape?" said Rachel to Silentwing.

"There is something you could do," he replied. "Help me to send Jack Frost away from the mountains. All the animals are scared of him. Whenever he comes here with his goblins, they hurt our home."

"What do they do?" Kirsty asked.

"They always leave trails of rubbish," said Silentwing. "They destroy plants and damage trees. Once they lit a fire and melted the snow. We make our nests in the snow, and many of our homes were ruined."

"We won't let them spoil your beautiful home," Selma promised. "But first we have to find them."

Side by side, the three fairies and the snowbird flew higher and higher into the Blue Ice Mountains. Their breath was misty in the cold air, but they felt snuggly warm in their snow-leopard onesies.

"Look down there," said Rachel, pointing to some marks in the snow. "Are those footprints?"

"Yes, goblin footprints," said Kirsty. "Lots of them! There must be a group of goblins somewhere nearby."

Silentwing swooped upwards and hovered high above them, gazing down on the mountains. Suddenly he plunged down again.

"I can see a fire," he said. "It's in the middle of our nesting place. Please hurry!"

Chapter Four
Fire Fighting

Rachel, Kirsty and Selma zoomed
after the snowbird. Silentwing led them
to a sheltered patch of snow. It was
underneath a rocky ledge, and there were
three goblins squatting around a blazing
fire. The snow was melting around them
in a wide circle.

"Put that out at once," said Selma, hovering in front of the goblins.

The goblins jumped up and stood in front of the fire, scowling. "No way!" one of them wailed. "We're freezing!"

"I'll give you fluffy suits with magical heat inside them," said Selma. "But you have to put out that fire."

"Fluffy suits do sound good," said the tallest goblin. "Do they come in green?"

But the shortest goblin shoved him aside.

"We're not taking anything from a fairy," he said, stamping a foot. "Jack Frost looks after us."

"You shouldn't even be in these mountains," said Rachel, fluttering forwards. "You live down in the valley, in Goblin Grotto."

"Oh, I wish I was back in my cosy little hut," said the third goblin, whose nose had turned red with cold.

"Jack Frost told us to wait here while he chased after that stupid overgrown kitten," snapped the shortest goblin. "So stop complaining and follow orders."

"You have to put out that fire," said Kirsty, joining Rachel and Selma. "You're destroying the homes of the snowbirds."

"So?" said the red-nosed goblin, shrugging his shoulders. "Why should I care about a bunch of silly birds?"

"How would you feel if a giant came along and stamped all over Goblin

Grotto?" Rachel asked.

"A giant?" squealed the tall goblin. "Where?"

"I'm scared of giants," wailed the red-nosed goblin.

He dived headfirst into a snow bank. All the

fairies could see of him were his warty heels.

"In the human world, snow leopards' habitats are getting smaller every day," said Selma. "I don't want the same problems to happen in Fairyland. If you care about the creatures that share our world, then we can all work together to keep it beautiful."

The tall goblin seemed to be listening, but the short goblin just pulled a face at her.

"You're talking gobbledygook," he said. "Animals don't matter, and I'm not taking a fluffy suit from any fairy. I don't care what colour it is."

43

Selma turned to Rachel and Kirsty with tears in her eyes.

"How can they be so mean?" she asked. "I don't know what else to say to make them listen."

"If they won't listen, then we will have to put out the fire ourselves," said Rachel. She flew over the top of the goblins who were blocking their way. Then she picked up a big armful of snow and plonked it on top of the fire. Kirsty quickly did the same. There was a hiss and a fizz, and then the fire was gone.

"Hey, you interfering fairies!" yelled the short goblin. "That fire was keeping me

nice and toasty."

"If you visit someone else's home, you should treat it with respect," said Selma. "This is the home of the snowbirds."

"I've had enough of this," said the taller goblin grumpily. "I'm fed up with snow leopards and all this white snow. I want Goblin Grotto and the grey ice and my nice little hut."

"I've still got a bit of Jack Frost's magic left," said the red-nosed goblin.

The goblins looked at each other and nodded. Then they held hands. There was a bright-blue flash, and the goblins disappeared.

"Thank goodness," said Selma.

Suddenly a voice echoed around the mountains.

"GOBLINS!"

"Oh dear," said Rachel. "That's Jack Frost."

Chapter Five
Jack Frost's Pet

"ANSWER ME, YOU TIRESOME THREESOME!" Jack Frost bellowed from somewhere above them.

His voice seemed to shake the mountain.

"Quickly," said Kirsty, turning to Selma. "Make me sound like a goblin."

Selma put her wand to Kirsty's throat and whispered a spell.

"Coming," Kirsty squawked.

"Well, hurry up about it," snapped Jack Frost. "I want to train this snow leopard to do tricks, and I need you lot to show it how."

"Oh, how can he?" demanded Selma in a rage. "Dotty isn't a toy or a game. She should be playing with her friends in Sparkle Forest. She must be so scared. I'm going to fly up there and tell exactly what I think of him."

"Hold on," said Rachel. "I think I have an idea. There were three goblins and there are three of us. If you can disguise us as goblins, maybe we can find a way to get Dotty away from him."

Selma tapped herself, Kirsty and

Rachel on the head with the tip of her wand. Instantly, they felt themselves change.

"It's like I'm hiding inside a goblin suit," said Rachel, laughing.

She jumped up and down a couple of times, leaving large footprints in the snow. Kirsty giggled and held her green hands out in front of her.

"Come ON!" Jack Frost bellowed.

The echo shook the mountain, and all the snow fell off the rocky ledge above them.

"You'll have to stay here," Kirsty said to Silentwing. "We promise we will do our best to get Jack Frost to leave your home alone."

"Thank you," said Silentwing. "And if you need help, just throw this into the air."

He shook his head, and one of the feathers fell from his crown into Kirsty's hand.

"Thank you," said Kirsty.

The three fairy-goblins
ran out from under the
ledge. A steep cliff rose
up in front of them. They
could see Jack Frost
peering over the top of it
with Dotty tucked under
his arm. There was a
lead attached to a collar
around her neck.

"We can't fly up," said
Kirsty. "Jack Frost is watching."

"How would the goblins get up there?"
Selma asked.

Suddenly, three ropes slithered down the
side of the cliff.

"Get climbing!" yelled Jack Frost.

"Without wings?" Selma gasped.

Rachel grinned at Kirsty.

"It's lucky we get so much practice in PE class," she said. "Don't worry, Selma. Just copy us and you'll be fine."

Slowly and steadily, they pulled themselves up the side of the cliff.

"It's much easier to climb with goblin hands and feet," said Kirsty.

When they pulled themselves over the top, Jack Frost was tapping his foot.

"Get up!" he bellowed at them. "Stop dawdling. Time to teach this overgrown pussycat a few tricks."

"May I cuddle her, please?" asked Selma.

Jack Frost gave a surprised frown, and Rachel nudged Selma with her elbow.

"Er, I mean, I want to hold her," said Selma, trying to sound as rude as a goblin.

"Tough," said Jack Frost. "You're too stupid to be able to control her. You don't know anything know about snow leopards."

"We do," said Kirsty, exchanging a glance with Rachel.

Their Tail and Trunk tour guide,

Ahmed, had told them lots of facts about snow leopards.

"Snow leopards like living on mountain ridges and cliffs," said Rachel.

"Rubbish," said Jack Frost. "In my zoo, she'll live in a dog kennel."

"They are shy and mysterious animals," said Kirsty.

"Not this one," said Jack Frost. "She will have to be on show all day long."

Selma couldn't say anything. She was upset by Jack Frost's plans, and she was worried about Dotty. The baby snow leopard had her eyes shut and her head down.

"You don't know about snow leopards," said Jack Frost. "Now get down on your hands and knees and show her how to chase a ball of string."

"Snow leopards don't chase balls of string," said Rachel.

"Oh, shut up," said Jack Frost. "You teach her a trick then, if you're so clever."

He put Dotty on the ground and held out the lead. Selma took a step forward. Then Dotty looked up. Her timid eyes

filled with trust and love, and Selma forgot all about the goblin disguise.

"Dotty, I'm so happy to see you," she exclaimed. "It's me, Selma!"

She waved her wand and her goblin disguise fell away.

Jack Frost snatched the lead back and glared at Selma.

"Pesky fairy!" he shouted, picking Dotty up again. "You're not getting her back!"

Chapter Six
A Pair of Cheeky Monkeys

Jack Frost waved his wand, and snow clouds started to swirl around him, faster and faster. At the same time, his magic made the goblin disguises fall away. A dark storm cloud lifted him off the ground and zoomed away.

"Chase him!" cried Rachel.

The fairies raced after the Ice Lord. He sent blue thunderbolts flying at them.

"I can't catch up with him," Rachel called, dodging thunderbolts left and right.

"Time to ask for some help," Kirsty replied. She threw the white snowbird feather into the air. For a moment, nothing happened.

"Did I do it wrong?" she wondered.

Then she heard something above
the noise of the rushing wind and the
thunderbolts. The fairies shared happy,
amazed smiles.

"It's music," said Rachel.

The next moment, a flock of snowbirds
swooped up from beneath them, led by
Silentwing. Their music was different
from anything the girls had ever heard
before.

"It's like Christmas and birthdays and

snow and sunshine all wrapped up into a song," said Kirsty.

The birds were quicker than the fairies. They started to fly around Jack Frost, faster and faster.

"I can't see!" shouted Jack Frost. "Clear off, you daft birds!"

He tried to flap them away, but the

snowbirds would not leave him. He slowed down and stopped. Still the birds swirled around him. He shut his eyes.

"He's dizzy," cried Selma. "This is our chance!"

She zoomed forwards and lifted Dotty out of his arms, pulling the collar from around her neck.

"Dotty," she said.

The snow leopard nuzzled into her neck. At once, the snowbirds rose up and scattered into the sky. Jack Frost saw Selma holding Dotty.

"You tricky fairies!" he yelled in a rage. "That's my snow leopard."

"Wild animals don't belong to anyone," said Rachel. "Dotty is free now."

"What about my private zoo?" Jack Frost wailed.

"You will not have it," said Kirsty, putting her hands on her hips. "You tried to harm the baby endangered animals,

and you failed. Go home, Jack Frost!"

Muttering under his breath, Jack Frost turned and flew away on his thunderbolt. As he left the mountains, Silentwing fluttered down and landed on Kirsty's arm.

"Thank you for sending them away," he said. "Our mountain home is safe again."

The fairies said goodbye to Silentwing, and then Selma waved her wand. In a flurry of twinkling fairy dust, the mountains, the snow and the fluffy onesies disappeared. They were standing in Sparkle Forest, surrounded by the smiling Endangered Animals Fairies. Snowy, Bobo and Stampy rushed forward to welcome Dotty.

"You did it," said Etta, putting her arms

around Rachel and Kirsty. "At last our forest feels magical again."

The fairies walked towards the glade arm in arm. They were followed by all the animals of the forest, from a prowling red wolf and a baby gorilla to a panda and a black-skinned rhinoceros munching on leaves.

"They're all safe, thanks to you," said Selma.

"That's the best reward," said Rachel, smiling.

"Now I think it's time for you to head back to Tail and Trunk," said Chelsea. "Your final morning is waiting for you."

"And now all the baby animals have been found, you can relax," added Priya.

"We'll miss you all," said Kirsty, hugging them all.

"Goodbye, Rachel and Kirsty!" called the Endangered Animals Fairies together. "Thank you!"

Selma waved her wand, and a bright

light dazzled Rachel and Kirsty. When
they could look again, they found
that they were back in their room in
the cabin, and the morning sun was
streaming through the curtains.

"Come on, girls," called Mr Walker
from the kitchen. "Ahmed will be here

soon, and I've made pancakes."

Rachel and Kirsty pulled on their clothes and went to have their breakfast. They had loved every minute of their time at the safari park, and they didn't want to miss their last morning with Ahmed. They really enjoyed putting out fresh straw and food for the animals.

"Which animals shall we ask to see?" said Rachel. "Meerkats? Monkeys?"

"I love them all," said Kirsty.

"Let's try to go and say goodbye to every animal we've met here," Kirsty suggested.

"That might take a while," said Rachel's dad, chuckling.

"I don't mind," said Rachel. "I'd love to live at the safari park, just like the elephants and the monkeys."

"Well, you'd fit right in," said Mr Walker. "When you two are giggling together, you're definitely a pair of cheeky monkeys."

The girls laughed.

"I love it here too," said Mrs Walker. "There's something really special about

the place."

"It's definitely the most magical safari park I've ever visited," said Kirsty.

"Me too," said Rachel, sharing a secret smile with her best friend. "And I hope that our next adventure together will be just as magical!"

The End

**Now it's time for Kirsty and
Rachel to help...**

Evelyn the
Mermicorn Fairy

Read on for a sneak peek...

"I love listening to the rain beating
on the window," said Rachel Walker.
"Especially when it's so cosy inside."

She snuggled deeper into her favourite
armchair and gazed into the flickering
flames of the fire. Her best friend, Kirsty
Tate, put down the pattern she was
stitching.

"Me too," she said.

Kirsty was spending the last week of the
holidays at Rachel's house in Tippington.
Although they went to different schools,

they saw each other as often as they could. They always had the best fun when they were together, and they often shared secret, magical adventures with their fairy friends.

The sitting room door opened and Rachel's dad popped his head around it.

"Anyone for hot chocolate?" he asked.

"Yes please," said the girls together.

"With whipped cream and sprinkles?" Rachel added.

"Of course," said Mr Walker. "Maybe it'll make up for not being able to go pebble collecting on the beach. What did you want the pebbles for?"

"We were going to paint inspiring pictures and messages on them, and then put them back on the beach for other people to find," Kirsty explained.

"But it's OK," said Rachel. "We found

something else crafty to do instead."

Her dad looked at the cross-stitch patterns they were holding. Kirsty was working on a turquoise mermaid with golden hair, and Rachel was stitching a snow-white unicorn.

"Those look complicated," he said.

"Yes, but it'll be a great feeling when they're finished," said Kirsty.

Mr Walker went to make the hot chocolate, and the girls carried on stitching.

"What's your favourite, mermaids or unicorns?" asked Rachel.

"I don't think I can choose," said Kirsty. "After all, we've met them both on our adventures, and they were just as magical and inspiring as each other."

Just then, they heard a tiny, tinkling giggle. The girls exchanged a surprised glance.

"That sounded exactly like a fairy," said Rachel.

There was another bell-like giggle, and the girls jumped to their feet.

"Where are you?" Kirsty asked.

Then Rachel noticed that her dark hair was sprinkled with sparkling fairy dust. Kirsty saw the same thing on Rachel's hair. They both looked up at the same time, and laughed out loud.

A chestnut-haired fairy was waving at them from the top of the round glass light pendant. She slid down it with a whoop and turned somersaults through the air, landing on the sofa arm with a bounce. She was wearing a shimmering, glittery blue skirt and a matching denim jacket.

"Hello," she said. "I'm Evelyn the Mermicorn Fairy."

"Hello, Evelyn," said Rachel, kneeling down in front of her. "What has brought you to my sitting room?"

"And what's a mermicorn?" Kirsty added.

"Exactly what it sounds like," said Evelyn with a smile. "It's the rarest, most magical creature in all of Fairyland – half mermaid and half unicorn."

"Oh, it sounds wonderful," said Kirsty in a whisper. "I wish I could see one."

"We only see them once a year," said Evelyn. "We always celebrate their visit with the Mermicorn Festival. That's why I'm here. Would you like to come and enjoy the festival with me?"

Rachel and Kirsty squealed in excitement.

"We'd love to," said Kirsty.

"Then it's time to go to Fairyland," said

Evelyn. Evelyn opened her hand, and the girls saw that she was holding a little pile of sparkling fairy dust.

"Don't you have a wand?" asked Rachel.

Evelyn smiled.

"Not today," she said.

She blew the fairy dust towards the girls, and a pastel rainbow swirled around them. Everything shimmered in light shades of blue, yellow, green and pink. Rachel and Kirsty reached for each other's hand as their delicate wings unfolded.

"Listen," said Kirsty. "The rain sounds different."

"Yes, I can't hear the raindrops spattering against the window any more," said Rachel. "It sounds more like … waves."

At that moment, the pastel-coloured swirl of fairy dust vanished away, and the girls found themselves sitting on a small stretch of golden sand.

"It *was* waves," said Kirsty in delight. "Yippee, we made to the beach after all."

"This is a bit more magical than the one I was planning to visit," said Rachel with a happy laugh.

"Welcome to Mermicorn Island," said Evelyn.

"I've never seen such fine sand," said Kirsty, letting it run through her fingers.

"Or such blue sea," Rachel added, cartwheeling down to the shore.

The sun was sparkling on the water, and it looked as if tiny diamonds were dancing in the waves. As Rachel turned around to smile at her best friend, she saw a beautiful sight. At the edge of the beach was a row of candy-coloured stalls, gleaming with a pearly sheen. Fairies were walking barefoot from stall to stall, wearing shells plaited into their hair and pearls threaded into necklaces and belts. The Music Fairies were playing an oceanic tune on driftwood instruments.

Read **Evelyn the Mermicorn Fairy** to find out what adventures are in store for Kirsty and Rachel!

Calling all parents, carers and teachers!
The Rainbow Magic fairies are here to help
your child enter the magical world of reading.
Whatever reading stage they are at, there's
a Rainbow Magic book for everyone!
Here is Lydia the Reading Fairy's guide to
supporting your child's journey at all levels.

Starting Out

1 Our Rainbow Magic Beginner Readers are perfect for first-time readers who are just beginning to develop reading skills and confidence. Approved by teachers, they contain a full range of educational levelling, as well as lively full-colour illustrations.

Developing Readers

2 Rainbow Magic Early Readers contain longer stories and wider vocabulary for building stamina and growing confidence. These are adaptations of our most popular Rainbow Magic stories, specially developed for younger readers in conjunction with an Early Years reading consultant, with full-colour illustrations.

Going Solo

3 The Rainbow Magic chapter books - a mixture of series and one-off specials - contain accessible writing to encourage your child to venture into reading independently. These highly collectible and much-loved magical stories inspire a love of reading to last a lifetime.

www.rainbowmagicbooks.co.uk

"Rainbow Magic got my daughter reading chapter books. Great sparkly covers, cute fairies and traditional stories full of magic that she found impossible to put down" - Mother of Edie (6 years)

"Florence LOVES the Rainbow Magic books. She really enjoys reading now" - Mother of Florence (6 years)

The Rainbow Magic Reading Challenge

Well done, fairy friend – you have completed the book!
This book was worth 5 points.

See how far you have climbed on the
Reading Rainbow opposite.

The more books you read, the more points you will get,
and the closer you will be to becoming a Fairy Princess!

How to get your Reading Rainbow
1. Cut out the coin below
2. Go to the Rainbow Magic website
3. Download and print out your poster
4. Add your coin and climb up the Reading Rainbow!

There's all this and lots more at
www.rainbowmagicbooks.co.uk

You'll find activities, competitions, stories, a special
newsletter and complete profiles of all the
Rainbow Magic fairies. Find a fairy with your name!